The Panda from Nana

Written by Baba Ma-Lewis
Illustrated by Yang Liu

For Lily, our sweet princess,
and those who explore all sorts of food.

For Neil, my dear husband,
and the parents who encourage our children to do so.

THE PANDA FROM NANA by BABA MA-LEWIS
Published by MA-LEWIS PRESS

ISBN: 978-988-75738-1-4
Printed in the U.S.
1st Edition

This book belongs to:

....

Lily lives with her two Dads, three cats, four rabbits, five horses, six ducks, seven squirrels and eight pigs on a farm.

Δ

Every morning, Lily's two Dads
work on the farm...

...and Lily plays with her friends.

One day, there was a ring at the door.

Was it Dada?
Was it Baba?
....

NO...

It was a **Panda,**

a huge, furry, black and white **Panda.**

"Hello, Lily," said the Panda.
"I am your birthday present from Nana."

"Do you have any food?" asked the Panda.

"Because I am very hungry after my long journey all the way from **China**."

Lily was puzzled for a second...

...and said: "Of course, here you go, a banana."

"I never had bananas before, but I will give it a go."

the panda ate the banana,
but he didn't like it.

"How about a fish?" meowed the cats.

"I never had fish before, but I will give it a go."

the Panda ate the fish, but he didn't like it.

"Maybe carrots?" squeaked the rabbits.

"I never had carrots before,
but I will give it a go."

the Panda ate the carrot,
but he didn't like it.

"We love grass, you should try it too."
neighed the horses.

"I never had grass before,
but I will give it a go."

the Panda ate some grass,
but he didn't like it.

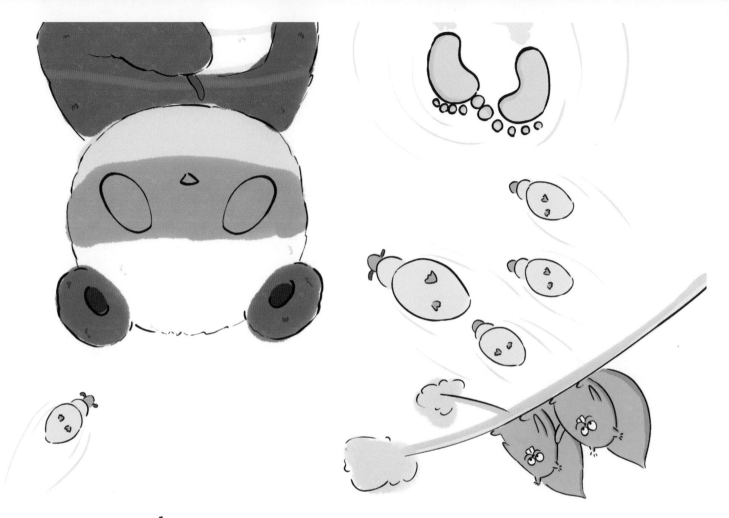

"What about **bugs**?" quacked the ducks.

"I never had bugs before,
but I will give them a go."

the Panda ate a few **bugs**,
but he didn't like them.

"Everyone loves nuts." squeaked the squirrels.

"I never had nuts before, but I will give them a go."

the Panda ate some nuts, but he didn't like them.

"Perhaps corn!" oinked the pigs.

"I never had corn before,
but I will give it a go."

the Panda ate some corn,
but he didn't like it.

"Ice cream?" Lily gave her favourite chocolate flavoured ice cream to the Panda.

"I never had ice cream before, but I will give it a go."

the Panda ate the ice cream, but he didn't like it.

"Grapes?" said Dada. "I never had grapes before, but I will give them a go."

the Panda ate some grapes, but he didn't like them.

"Maybe you will like **watermelon**." suggested Baba.

"I never had watermelon before,
but I will give it a go."

the Panda ate the **watermelon**,
but still, he didn't like it.

The Panda tried all the food in the house...

...and all the **vegetables** on the farm,

...and all the food that the Cats, Rabbits, Horses, Ducks, Squirrels and Pigs like,

... and all the food that Lily, Dada and Baba could **think** of.

Still, he couldn't find the food that he likes, but they didn't give up.

"How about these?"
Lily saw bamboo in the garden.

"I never had those before,
but I will give them a go."

The Panda ate one **bamboo** root,
then a bamboo shoot,
and then one bamboo leaf,
then another leaf.......

Until a big bamboo bush was gone.

"I love eating bamboo."
burped the Panda.

BURP

"Hooray!"
Everyone cheered, they finally found
what the Panda likes to eat the most,

...and what's more, the Panda was no longer just black and white, he had become the most colourful panda in the entire world.

Avaiable on Amazon,
Barnes & Noble and other major online bookstores

A Sunday with My 2 Dads

Story of Lily
Written by Baba Mr-Lewis
Illustrated by Dada

ISBN: 978-988-75738-3-8

While Lily and her doggyGo-go were ready for their family adventure on this Sunday morning, her two Dads were still sleeping......

Printed in Great Britain
by Amazon

84340417R00018